SOUTHERN
OKLAHOMA
Library System

D1317296

WITHDRAWN FROM
SOUTHERN OKLAHOMA
LIBRARY SYSTEM

WITHDRAWN FROM
SOUTHERN OKLAHOMA
LIBRARY SYSTEM

This edition published by Parragon Books Ltd in 2014 and distributed by

Parragon Inc.
440 Park Avenue South, 13th Floor
New York, NY 10016
www.parragon.com

Copyright © 2014 Disney Enterprises, Inc.

All rights reserved. No part of this publication may be reproduced, stored in a retrieval system or transmitted, in any form or by any means, electronic, mechanical, photocopying, recording or otherwise, without the prior permission of the copyright holder.

ISBN 978-1-4723-4156-3

Printed in China

The Flower Mystery

Read the story, then turn over the book
to read another story!

Disney
MINNIE

The Flower Mystery

PaRragon

Bath · New York · Cologne · Melbourne · Delhi
Hong Kong · Shenzhen · Singapore · Amsterdam

One spring day, Daisy Duck rang Minnie Mouse's doorbell.
"Hi, Minnie," Daisy said. "I brought you some marigolds from
my garden."

"Daisy, you're a dear!" said Minnie. "They'll look perfect with my daffodils."

"Definitely," Daisy agreed. "Daffodils are my favorite flowers."

"Mine, too," said Minnie. But when the friends went out to Minnie's backyard, they had a big surprise.

"My daffodils!" Minnie wailed. "They're gone!"

"What happened?" Minnie cried. "They were here yesterday!"

"The stems are still here," Daisy pointed out.

Minnie looked more closely. "You're right," she said. "But the flowers are missing. It looks like they've been chopped off!"

"This is terrible," Daisy said. "Someone must have taken them!"

"What's this?" Daisy asked a moment later. She pulled
a few strands of fuzzy white hair off a bush near the
daffodil patch.

"Is it a clue?" Minnie asked.

"Maybe," Daisy said. "But it could just be from Fluffy's bow."

A moment later,
Minnie's doorbell rang.
Mickey Mouse was
standing on the porch.

"Hi, Minnie," he said
shyly. "I brought you a
present." He held out
a big bunch of daffodils
tied with a fluffy white
ribbon!

"Oh, no! Mickey, you
cut down my daffodils!"
Minnie cried.

"What do you mean, Minnie?" Mickey exclaimed.
"I bought these at Power's Flower Shop because I know
daffodils are your favorite flowers!"

Minnie smiled. "Really?" she said. She was glad that Mickey had not taken her flowers.

Minnie, Daisy, and Mickey decided to look for clues around town. They headed to the park and found Goofy—wearing a daffodil! And he was playing with a yo-yo that had a fuzzy white string!

"Gawrsh, Minnie," Goofy said. "I didn't do it. This daffodil came from Power's Flower Shop. Mr. Power is having a sale on daffodils today."

"Really?" Minnie said. "That's quite a coincidence."

Daisy nodded. "Maybe we'd better check out Mr. Power's flowers. Right now!"

The four friends went to Power's Flower Shop.
They peeked in the window.
"That's Mr. Power," Mickey said.

Minnie saw that the shopkeeper had a sharp pair of scissors, a fuzzy white mustache, and a shop full of daffodils!

"He did it!" she cried. "I know it!"

Minnie and her friends entered the shop. "Where did
you get these daffodils?" Minnie asked.

"From a farmer named Mrs. Pote," Mr. Power answered.
"She delivers daffodils here every day. But today she
brought dozens of extras!"

"Could Mrs. Pote have taken my daffodils?"
Minnie wondered. "Where can we find her?"
she asked.

Mr. Power pointed. "That way," he said.
"You can't miss her. She has fuzzy white hair."

Mrs. Pote's farm was called Pote's Goats. "Yes, I delivered extra daffodils today," Mrs. Pote told Minnie. "My favorite goat, Flower, usually eats a lot of them as soon as they bloom. But today she didn't seem very hungry."

That gave Minnie an idea. "May I see Flower?" she asked.
Mrs. Pote led the friends to a pen. But there was no goat
inside! "Oh, dear!" Mrs. Pote cried. "She must have escaped!"

"Look! There's a hole in the fence," Mickey said, pointing.

"Now what do we do?" Daisy exclaimed. "Not only are Minnie's daffodils gone, but so is Mrs. Pote's goat!"

"Hmmm," said Minnie, deep in thought. "Maybe these two mysteries are connected!"

"What do you mean, Minnie?" Daisy asked.

"I think I know who took my flowers," Minnie explained. "It's someone who really likes daffodils. Someone who likes them even more than we do!"

Daisy held up the fuzzy strands of white hair.
"Don't forget this," she reminded Minnie. "Isn't it a clue?"
"It sure is," Minnie agreed. "And so is this!" She pointed
toward a trail of footprints. "Just follow me!"

Minnie and the others followed the footprints straight to
Daisy's backyard. There was Flower, happily munching away.
"See?" Minnie said. "I knew it! There's the little scamp.
Now, if we could only train her to like weeds instead!"

The End

Now turn over the book
for another classic Disney tale!

Now turn over the book
for another classic Disney tale!

The End

The footprints finally disappeared beneath Daisy's bed. Mickey kneeled down and peeked underneath. "Oh, Pluto," sighed Mickey, as a guilty-looking dog with butterscotch crumbs all over his mouth came out from under the bed.

Pluto let out a groan.

Minnie just smiled. "Don't be too tough on him, Mickey," she said, giving Pluto a pat on the head. "It looks as if he has quite a tummy ache!"

"Come on," Minnie cried. "Let's find out who the mischief-maker is!" She and her friends followed the trail of footprints across the kitchen, up the stairs, and into Daisy's bedroom.

"Hey, Minnie," called Mickey. "I found some
footprints." He pointed at the floor.

Minnie decided to trust Donald. After all, she didn't have any proof that he had taken them.

"Come on," she said. "Let's go to the kitchen and look for clues."

The five friends went out to the kitchen and started their search.

Minnie wasn't sure whether or not to believe him. Donald liked to eat almost as much as Goofy did. And he had unwrapped the package. Was he telling the whole truth?

Donald was looking more and more anxious. When Minnie turned to him, he squawked, "It wasn't me! It wasn't me!"

Daisy gave him a suspicious stare. "Are you sure, Donald?"

Donald nodded vigorously. "I, um, might have smelled them," he said nervously. "I even might have unwrapped the foil to take a peek. But I absolutely, positively did not taste your brownies—not one crumb!"

"How could you unwrap the foil package with both of your thumbs bandaged?"

Goofy held up his thumbs, looking relieved. "Gawrsh, I couldn't," he agreed.

Goofy gulped nervously. "I sneaked out to the kitchen once when no one was looking," he admitted. "I ate a few things, but I didn't touch that bag."

Minnie looked at him thoughtfully, before she realized something. "You couldn't have done it, Goofy," she said.

"It wasn't me," Mickey said quickly. "You and I have been dancing since you got here, Minnie. I haven't been near the kitchen."

"That's true," Minnie said. "You couldn't have taken the butterscotch brownies. But if it wasn't you and it wasn't Daisy, then who was it?"

"Yup," Goofy agreed. "Donald always gets butterscotch sundaes when he goes to the ice cream shop with Daisy so he won't have to share. That doesn't work when he's with me, though," he added, rubbing his belly.

"I guess that proves you didn't take them, Daisy," Minnie said. "So who did?"

"I didn't take your brownies, Minnie," Daisy said. "I don't even like butterscotch."

"Really?" Minnie said. "I didn't know that."

Mickey laughed. "Everybody knows that Daisy would rather eat spinach than butterscotch," he said.

Goofy shrugged. "I wish I had," he said sadly.
"But I haven't."

"Well, someone must have taken them," said Minnie.
"They were in this bag when I got here. One of you must
have slipped out to the kitchen and gobbled down every
last bite!"

Minnie went back to the living room. "My brownies are missing!" she cried, waving the empty bag in the air. "I haven't seen them!" said Daisy, Donald, and Mickey, one after the other, as they shook their heads.

Minnie looked all around the kitchen, but the butterscotch brownies were gone!

Minnie ran to the kitchen. But when she got there, she had a big surprise. The shopping bag was tipped over on the table— and there was nothing inside but some crumbs and foil.

"The butterscotch brownies!" she exclaimed. "I brought some for
the party, but I forgot to unpack them."

"Well, what are you waiting for?" asked Goofy, hungrily licking
his lips. "Let's eat!"

Minnie was still dancing with Mickey half an hour later when she suddenly remembered the treats she had brought.

"Gosh, I'm happy you're here, Minnie," said Mickey, with a shy smile. "Would you like to dance?"

"I'd love to," Minnie said, leaving her shopping bag on the kitchen table and following Mickey to the living room.

When Minnie arrived at Daisy's house, the other guests were already there. Daisy was taking a platter of food out of the refrigerator while Donald Duck looked on hungrily. Goofy, who was wearing bandages on both thumbs, was carefully petting Mickey Mouse's dog, Pluto.

"I was trying to hang up some pictures," Goofy explained to Minnie. "But I sorta missed—twice."

"Delicious!" Minnie Mouse said, taking a tiny taste of a butterscotch brownie. She had just baked a whole batch of the tasty treats for Daisy Duck's party. "The gang will just love these!" she said to herself, as she wrapped the brownies in foil and tucked the package into her pretty pink shopping bag.

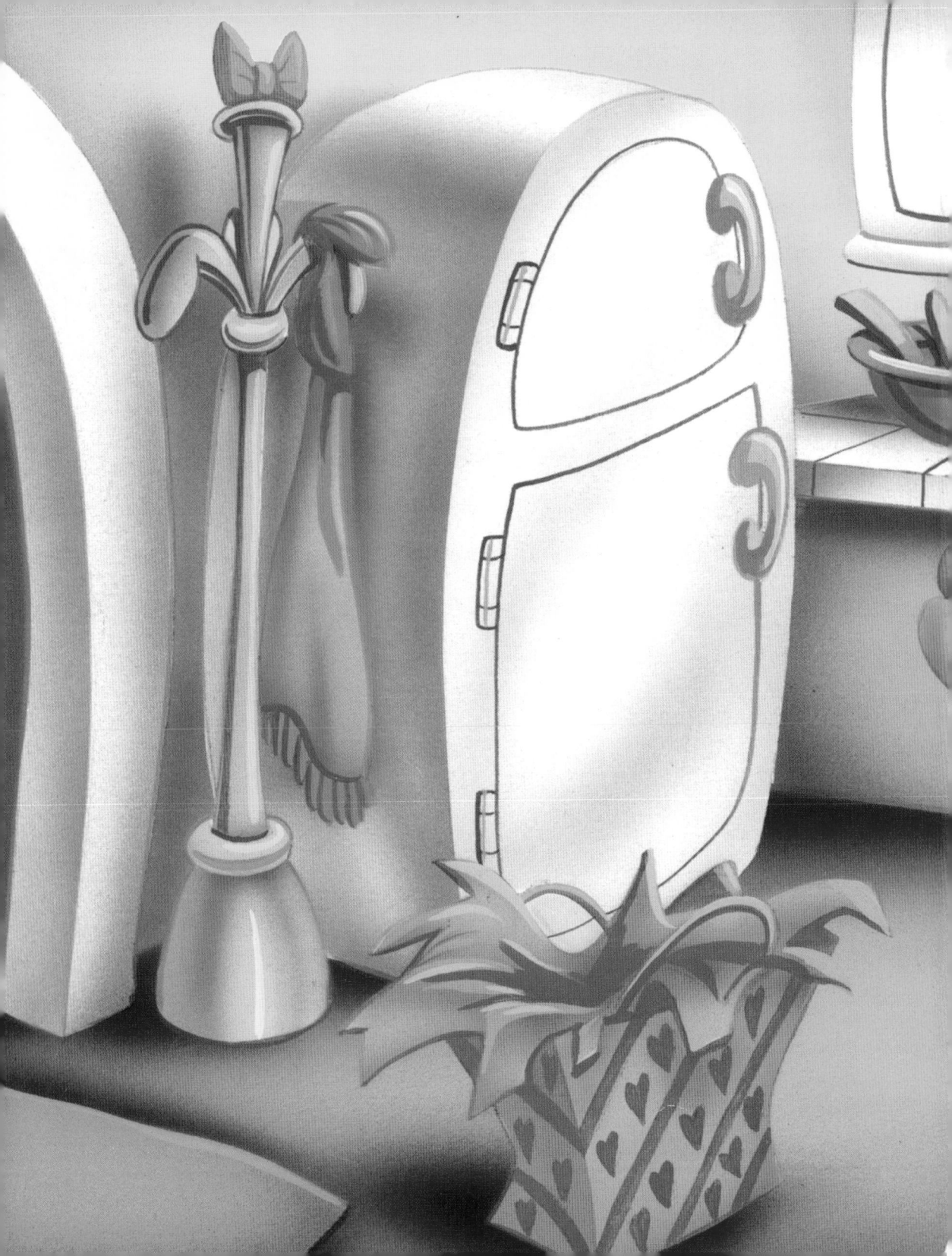

The Disappearing Dessert

PaRRagon

Bath · New York · Cologne · Melbourne · Delhi
Hong Kong · Shenzhen · Singapore · Amsterdam

The Disappearing Dessert

Read the story, then turn over the book
to read another story!

This edition published by Parragon Books Ltd in 2014 and distributed by

Parragon Inc.
440 Park Avenue South, 13th Floor
New York, NY 10016
www.parragon.com

Copyright © 2014 Disney Enterprises, Inc.

All rights reserved. No part of this publication may be reproduced, stored in a retrieval
system or transmitted, in any form or by any means, electronic, mechanical, photocopying,
recording or otherwise, without the prior permission of the copyright holder.

ISBN 978-1-4723-4156-3

Printed in China